More likely, when you hear the word "d
think of a small, but proper dog.
Perhaps the same as Stephan, a very
happy Jack Russell puppy.

Here are a few episodes of Stephan's very first
year of his life.

First of all, I have to tell the truth: Stephan can't write. To be honest I once gave him a pen to see what he would do, even hoped that he may have some hidden talents. But he simply chewed it.

His inability or unwillingness to write doesn't make him stupid or lazy, or anything in this range that we usually think about those who don't fit our conceptions. I don't know how to explain his strange behaviour...
He is quite smart.

So, I decided to investigate his denying of required writing later and, meanwhile, began to set down his diary myself.

Perhaps, my descriptions do not exactly reflect what Stephan would mean, if he could write himself, but I tried my best.

Here is Stephan on his very first morning in the new place.

Yesterday he left his Mum at the farm in Wales where he
was born and spent his two "baby" months.
We drove for long hours and all the way Stephan was
peacefully sleeping in the front seat of my car until very
late we finally arrived at my home in West London.

The next few days, Stephan was very busy.

He had to go around his new home, exploring every corner and trying to figure out why he had been taken away from his Mum.

There should be a reason for that!

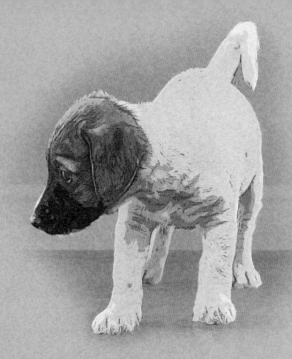

Stephan ran around in
the house and the backyard,
putting his nose everywhere
he could and sniffing and
tasting all the things he could
find and reach.
But he didn't find the answer.

OK, at least the place was
generally fine and safe.
I guess he found it acceptable
for living.

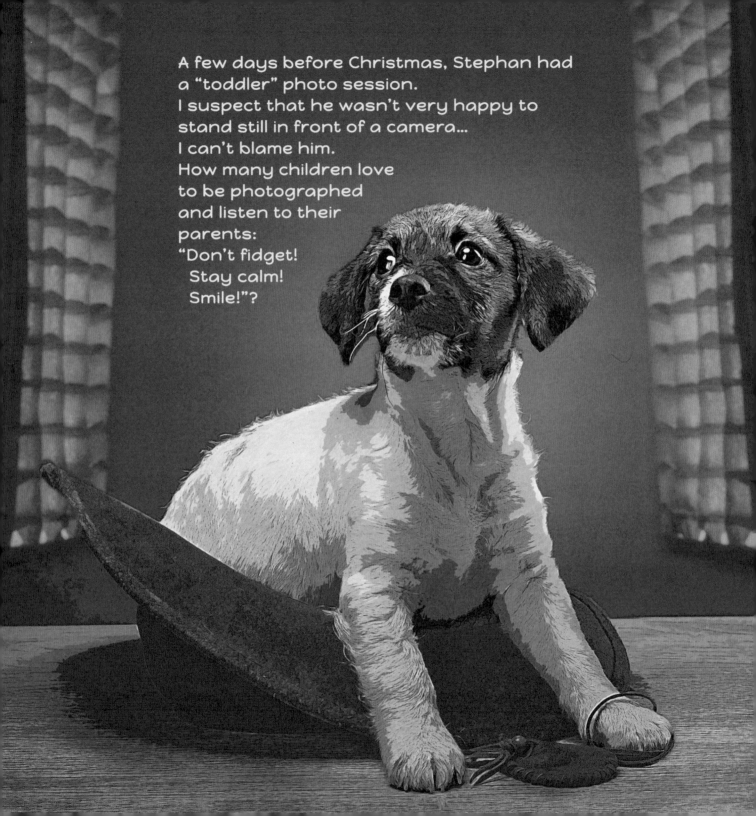

A few days before Christmas, Stephan had
a "toddler" photo session.
I suspect that he wasn't very happy to
stand still in front of a camera...
I can't blame him.
How many children love
to be photographed
and listen to their
parents:
"Don't fidget!
  Stay calm!
  Smile!"?

But since we were already having had the session, Stephan also got a few nice shots for greeting post cards for his friends.

Of course, I insisted on this and Stephan, as an obedient boy, agreed that it was better to do this now, not to delay until later.

He was exhausted but finally free to go...

The first month from his arrival, Stephan had to stay at home due to his vaccination. It makes sense if you don't want your child to get chickenpox.

Anyone can be scared. It is important to deal with your fear. But Stephan was born a daredevil!

The day, when he first went out,
he got shocked and surprised.
The open world was huge and
not as simple as his house.

Stephan even got scared.

Not for long though.

Very soon, Stephan met Hera,
a Dutch Shepherd dog.
They played, and played,
and played...

Obviously, from the first
moment they met they
liked each other.

I believe Stephan even fell in love with Hera.
Perhaps he would deny it if someone asked
him the straight question.

Stephan couldn't think of any better way to express his feelings and just started attacking Hera.
He behaved like a school boy who is pulling the pigtails of a girl he likes.

All boys are the same!

At four months old, Stephan had his first and unexpected swimming lesson.

That day he went to Black Park and had some fun playing around a lake. He was running after a wooden stick and bringing it back.

Suddenly, a gust of wind caused a stick to fall into the lake, out of reach off the shore.

Stephan ran after it, and because he had never seen water before, jumped on what he thought was smooth and solid ground...

And, surprisingly for him, sank under
water, making a lot of splashes.
But right away he got on
the surface, started to swim
and managed to get
ashore himself.

He proved that he
is a really tough guy!

One day, Stephan had a real challenge and, for a short time, got scared and even lost his confidence.

He met a really huge animals who were not very friendly to him.

However, from a distance,
the cows didn't look big
at all and Stephan perhaps
suggested that if he came
closer he could play
with them.

Fortunately, after being stressed by these cows,
he found a friendly and calm fox and got his
peace of mind back.

This exercise is called
"auto training".
So, Stephan was learning
how to handle difficult
situations.

Stephan's closest friend became Bundash, or for short, Bundi, an intelligent, I would even call him aristocratic, Dachshund dog.

Bundi is the closest, not only due to their relationship, but also because he is a neighbour and lives just behind a fence in the house next to Stephan's.

Bundi loves to play with Stephan and he comes to see Stephan very often, sometimes a few times a day.

Besides, they travel together a lot.
They visit parks and go to the forest for walks and to collect mushrooms.
Their friendship deserves a separate story.

Here is Maizie, one of Stephan's best friends. Maizie's favourite thing is to play with Stephan's ears, which she loves to bite, chew and pull out of Stephan's head.

Stephan takes all this with great patience.

However, when Maizie gets tired of this activity, she switches to chasing squirrels in trees.

But this girl has a brave heart and, and in challenging situations, Maizie is always on the right side.

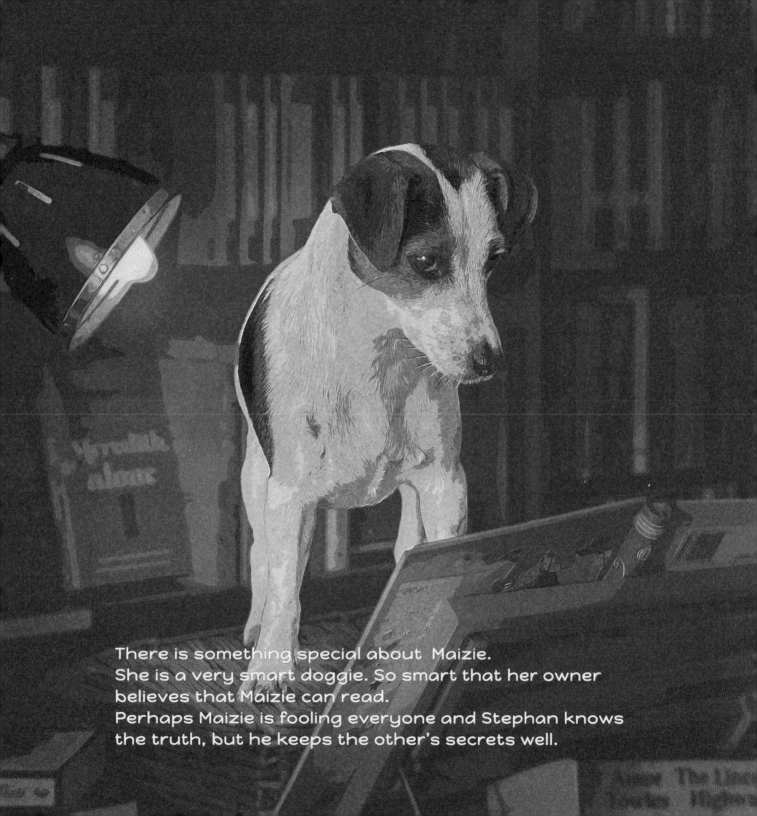

There is something special about Maizie.
She is a very smart doggie. So smart that her owner
believes that Maizie can read.
Perhaps Maizie is fooling everyone and Stephan knows
the truth, but he keeps the other's secrets well.

Stephan loves to swim.
Therefore, one of his favourite
places is the park at Virginia
Waters, because of its
huge lake.

Also, the park has many
other wonderful things
which make Stephan
amazed by and admire.

Such as the enormous
sized grass or a totem
pole which made him
speechless or, shall
we say, "barkless".

Nothing is better for Stephan on a hot sunny day than playing in the water, cooling himself and having a lot of fun!

Stephan loves the forest,
always ready to go there,
whatever the weather is
outside, and he is always into
discovering everything
around him to gain
more experience.

However, when gaining
experience, keep in mind
that this process is
usually not really pleasant.

How about putting a nose into
an anthill and making ants angry?
Ops!..
Yes, gaining experience may
be quite painful!

I guess Stephan learned the lesson.
It was definitely not the best way to get smarter.

One day, another of Stephan's friends, Koukou, came to visit Stephan and lived with him for three weeks while her owner was in a hospital.

During those days they both had an amazing time walking, playing and travelling together.

Their best and happiest times were when they were running in a forest, chasing each other, trying to win a race with a wooden stick as a trophy.

Unfortunately, Koukou's owner had passed away and Koukou had to move into a new home far away from Stephan.

But Stephan knows that one day they will meet again.

Friends must stay together.

It's Ben. Or "handsome" Ben.
That is how this Stephan's friend
likes to be named, I guess.

However, the value of friendship is not about how pretty you look but who you really are. Therefore, Ben even became Stephan's soul mate for a proper hike they had in Dorset.

Ben is really big, but sometimes he perhaps wishes to be a little bit smaller to play like others in the game.

During the first year of his life in London, Stephan made many good friends.

Some of them were visiting him to spend a very nice time together.

While Koukou stayed with Stephan, she also helped him to welcome every friend, especially Bundi, who was the most frequent visitor.

Good friends are always
ready to get into any game.

On Stephan's birthday we went to a park...
One year ago, I brought Stephan from Wales only
knowing that everything in our lives was going
to change.
At that time, I had no idea that I had taken home
my best ever buddy.

After a long day full of games, runs, chasing, barking,
sniffing and so on, Stephan went to his bed, getting
ready to sleep.
I hope Stephan's day went as happily as he deserved
and as his every other day should be.

And I also had the thought: everyone needs a dog.

P.S.

At the beginning of this diary I doubted Stephan's
intention to work hard on this book.
But recently, thanks to a dog's anatomy atlas
I found on the internet, I spotted, and can confirm,
that Stephan is unable to hold a pen in his paw
as we do in our hand.
It explains a lot, and I've thought that it's perfectly
fine to have a normal dog.
We wouldn't be very happy to live with a flying pig
or a talking horse...
Wouldn't we?

Printed in Great Britain
by Amazon

36481302R00021